K-1 PUBLISHING
K1Publishing.com

SOLUTIONIST
Vol. 1 Demonic Council

# SOLUTIONIST

## Also By Kayvan

K$_1$ PUBLISHING

Presents

SOLUTIONIST

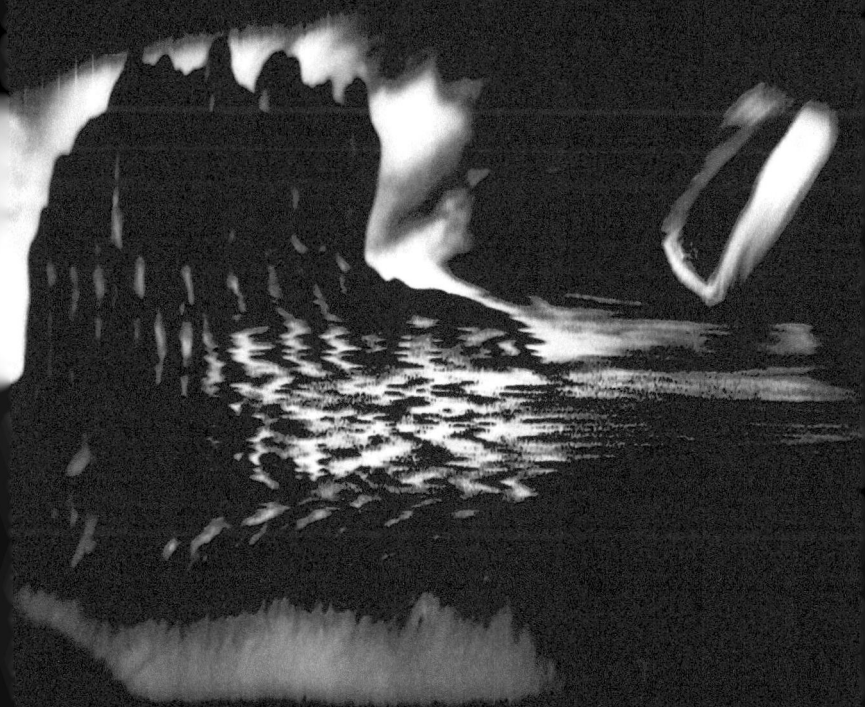

# Tribute

*I* dedicate this book to a kid with a great heart, a truly remarkable human being, who worked as a barista in a café where I practically wrote this novel. Amongst hundreds of baristas that I got to know during the three years of writing, Kevin was the only one who had maximum popularity with all his customers; cops, nurses, shopkeepers, writers, and entrepreneurs. They all loved him. He was everyone's guy and wasn't a phony. He knew each customer's name and drink. The second that they stepped into the shop, he greeted them by name and started to make their drink, while they were waiting in line. He loved his customers and they loved him back; a true rock star of the neighborhood.

One day he told me, "You must dedicate your book to me." I asked him why, and he replied with a grin, "Because I make the best soy foam!"

Sadly, Kevin passed away at the early age of 26. This book, as he requested, is dedicated to him.

# SOLUTIONIST
# V.
# SATAN

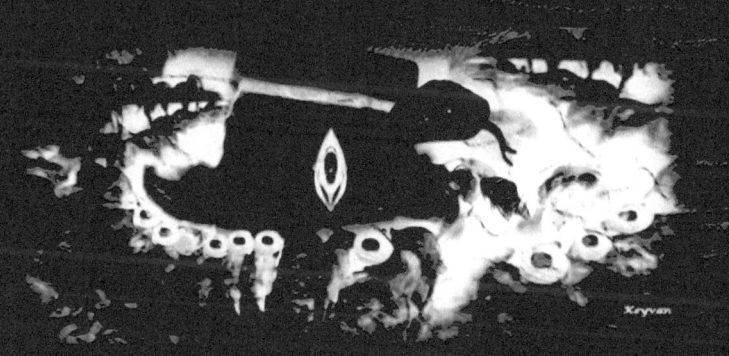

## VOL. I

## DEMONIC COUNCIL

Published in the United States of America
First Edition, 2014
*Book cover, design, and illustrations, created by Kayvan D.*

ISBN-10: 0986078018
ISBN-13: 978-0-9860780-1-9

FB.com/PersianFire
KayvanD.com
twitter.com/KayvanTweet

# Contents

# SOLUTIONIST

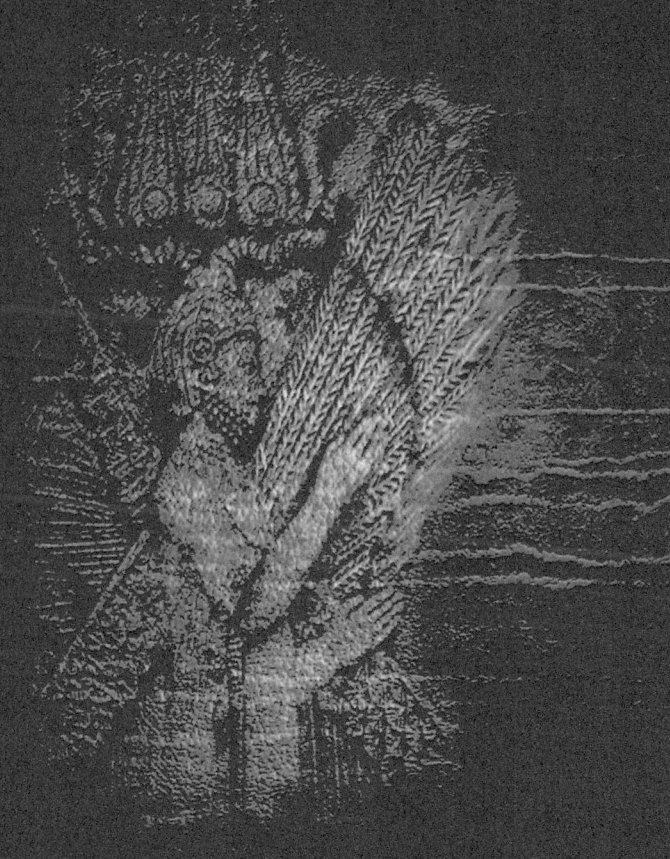

## A TRILOGY
## BY KAYVAN

Chapter **I**

## THE **BIRTH**

The **Persian Plateau, Anshan Desert**

### 605 BC

*I*n the dead of night, Ahuramazda (God) — eternal Lord of the Overworld and the Universe — selected a unique plateau for an unparalleled event. The landmark stood tall and powerful in a virgin valley nestled in the Zagros Mountains, where the desert lay barren, walled by the desolate mountains and roofed by the scintillating stars of the Milky Way Galaxy. Chilling breezes swept through the valley. The sleepy night seemed like any other, yet it was not. The distressed screams of a pregnant woman shredded the curtain of desert silence and echoed in the valley.

Ahriman, (Satan) Master of all Demons and the Underworld, appeared as an immense, hideous creature: a black, hunchbacked python, his long neck joined to the legless torso of a giant desert rat that sat like a hump on his back, trailing off into a serpentine rattle. His heavy body pushed against the sand, leaving behind a track that was deep and wide enough for a flock of sheep to pass through. He sought out the screaming woman, unaware that he was slithering into the path of a lurking killer.

Far faraway from the heart of the Milky Way Galaxy, a celestial phenomenon—similar in appearance to a shooting star raced toward Earth with astonishing speed. It had a long, golden tail of red iron dust. The closer it came to Earth, the brighter it became.

The woman screamed louder as her pain intensified.

The celestial phenomenon entered Earth's orbital plane and was caught in its gravitational field. It entered the atmosphere in a spectacular fashion, screeching earthward with an earsplitting whistle.

Atmospheric resistance caused it to ignite into a fireball.

The pregnant woman's agony increased.

Her screams blasted out.

Any moment now!

Ahriman sensed the object moving in the sky. He stopped in his tracks, looked up and saw the fireball. He assumed it would burn itself out and pursued the woman's pain-filled cries.

She let out a long, piercing scream and then stopped as the cries of another entered the world.

The birth!

The newborn's cries mixed with his mother's howl, which still reverberated between the walls of the valley.

The whistling of the fireball became deafening and drowned out the echoes of the mother and child.

Ahriman realized that the object would crash to Earth.

He was perplexed. Should he investigate the newborn on the mountain, or watch out for the fireball?

He moved his head from side to side, scanning the mountains and the sky.

In a flash, he saw a baby, sitting at the edge of a cliff, pointing to the sky. Ahriman looked up to see the fireball homing in on the very spot that he was patrolling, descending rapidly. It generated a wave of mega energy that caused the entire valley to tremble, illuminating the desert brighter than daylight. It looked like a piece of the sun falling to Earth. The earthquake became more violent.

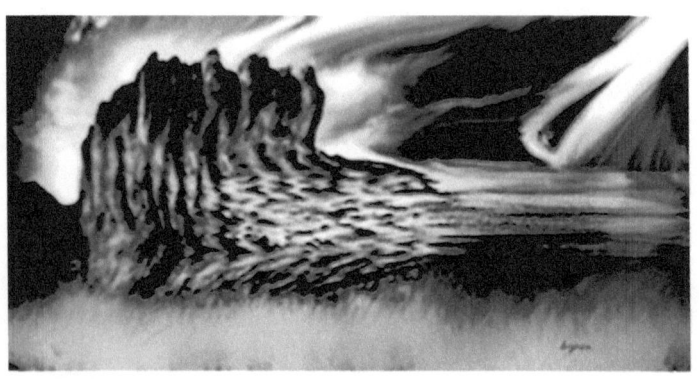

Gravel and stones collapsed from all of the surrounding mountains, save one. It was the rock save one. It was the rock where the baby had appeared earlier. Ahriman noticed that the cliff had not collapsed, but instead had propelled itself horizontally like a cluster of cannon balls, as if the cliff had tried to reshape itself.

He suspected that Ahuramazda had orchestrated the entire spectacle, and that the baby and his mother were merely an illusion.

A storm of dust and fiery stones rained down.

The celestial object was seconds away from impact.

Ahriman grabbed his tail in his mouth and coiled himself, morphing into black smoke and sinking himself into the sand.

The cosmic collision took place.

Its shockwave slammed into the ground with a blast of hot air, shattering the mountains like pulverized icebergs and blowing them away.

The impact decimated the landscape and caused a colossal dust storm.

Time passed.

Total silence descended.

Nothing to see.

Nothing to hear.

———

Chapter **II**

## TOWER OF SILENCE

The **Aryan Plateau, Proto-Elamite**

━━━━━━━━━━━━━━━━━━━━━━━━

**1600 BC**

*A*t the end of the Ice Age, as a result of extensive flooding, the Aryans had migrated from north of the Caspian Sea to the Alborz and Zagros Mountains, and formed what would become the Proto-Elamite. They were the vanguards of Planet Earth's civilization and the founders of the world's first empire: The Elamites.

A thousand years went by. Territorial and supremacy wars were waged, and the division began. The Elamite Empire split up and their descendants became the forebears of three kingdoms: the Parthians, the Persians, and the Medians. In 600 BC, these kingdoms were in their infancy.

Outside the Aryan Plateau, there were other realms: the Assyrians, Egyptians, Lydians, and

Athenians. They were distinct cultures that all followed pagan gods.

Only the Aryans, through the teaching of Zoroaster, practiced monotheism and worshiped Ahuramazda. He had only three rules: good thoughts, good words, good deeds — that was the definition of being a Zoroastrian. Fire was sacred and the temples had perpetual flames burning in them.

Zoroastrians did not cremate their dead, since they believed that the corpses would corrupt the fire. Burial was out of the question since, by their lore, graves were the access to the Underworld and the dominion of Ahriman, the Spirit of Destruction and Lord of the Darkness. The Zoroastrian tradition was to move their dead to Dakhma or the Tower of Silence, erected on the apex of a small hill. The bodies were left on the rooftop of the Tower to feed the birds of the sky, a process that was completed in a matter of hours: the humans' last contribution to nature.

Ahriman had set himself the most enduring mission of overriding Ahuramazda's three rules. He vowed to subdue all humans, particularly women, under his scourge and to purge Planet Earth of mankind altogether. To achieve this, in 1800 BC he developed a toxic elixir, with the poison to paralyze humans' faculty for thinking and understanding for themselves, and put them at the mercy of his agents, who would do the thinking for them. In this way he would gain mastery of the planet in the most vicious way possible, something happened and his first elixir was malpractice.

In retaliation to his second elixir and unbeknownst to Ahriman, Ahuramazda had prepared an antidote, capable of three thousand years of striking back at Ahriman and his agents from the Tower of Silence.

Chapter **III**

# CITADEL OF THE IMMORTALS

The **Persian Plateau, Anshan Desert**

## 605 BC

Shortly after the impact, through the thick layer of hovering dust, the black smoke rose above the sand and gradually morphed itself into the hunchbacked python. Ahriman surfaced and scanned the site. A devastating change was revealed to him.

The valley was no more.

The mountains were blown away.

Only one single cliff survived — the one with the baby.

As the cloud of dust settled and the air cleared, Ahriman realized the landmark had changed into a citadel: the Citadel of the Immortals.

The single cliff was revealed to be more than the rough rock it had previously been. The propelled stones had carved three giant square crosses, aligned next to one another. Within each cross, there was an open door to a tomb. The entrance to each tomb was at the center of each cross, opening into a small chamber.

On the ground, the cosmic impact had excavated a vast crater.

Ahriman realized he was inside the crater, and he was not alone. In its center was a mysterious, flaming object.

The infant chortled!

Flabbergasted, Ahriman looked up and saw the newborn still alive inside the center cross; he had his umbilical cord attached to the chamber's door and tethered as he was, the infant crawled toward the ledge of the cross.

Ahriman's mind was a turmoil of questions. 'Who is this baby? How did he survive the impact? Where is his mother? How can he crawl at birth? Why is his cord so long?'

As the hurricane of questions flew through his mind, the infant stopped at the edge of the cross and pointed at the flaming object. The instant he pointed at it, the fire mysteriously extinguished itself.

Ahriman had no doubt that the infant and the celestial object were somehow linked.

"But how?" he asked himself.

It had been a dangerous night so far, and things had just begun. The main menace might still lie ahead.

A deathly silence reigned over the site. Ahriman began to ponder the situation. Three moves stood before him. The first was extremely tempting: to slither towards the infant and investigate him, but the infant appeared surreal. Ahriman knew that no matter how believable an illusion was, it was still an illusion. Therefore, he rejected the first option. On the other hand, the celestial object was physically there. The alarming thought rooted in his mind was that the object might be more than a shooting star - it could be a living thing. That brought him to the second alternative, which was to go and inspect the object.

"Risky?" he mumbled to himself.

This wasn't his realm. The Aryans were followers of Ahuramazda, and this landmark was theirs. Maybe the object was for them? Ahriman decided against this second choice as well, instead turning his attention to the final alternative — withdrawing into the Underworld and maintaining a proud silence. He immediately rejected this as being a sign of cowardice. He was trapped in his own web. This was his area of expertise — tempting humans into irresistible misdeeds, and now Ahuramazda was making him taste his own medicine. He thought again. For all he knew, the object could just be a shooting star and the baby simply an illusion. He decided to choose the second option, to investigate the celestial object.

Ahriman stretched to his full length and undulated slowly and guardedly toward the object. Up close, it was completely different from what he had expected. It was a meteoroid, but an odd one. It was shaped meticulously into the form of a giant iron pyramid, which was now buried upside-down in the dirt. The other anomaly was the shiny, silvery liquid dripping out of fissures on its surface. Pensively,

Ahriman started to shake his rattle, its noise the only sound in the looming desert. He waited and thought. He was perplexed. Finally, he decided to analyze the conundrum. He stuck out his tongue cautiously and tasted the fluids that were on the sand. Immediately he spat it out.

"A pyramid full of mercury?"

Ahriman waited watchfully. He glanced back at the cross to check on the infant; the baby had vanished. He peered at the other two crosses, but the infant wasn't there either.

"Why has Ahuramazda orchestrated such a complex and peculiar phenomenon?"

As he contemplated the crosses, a thunderous explosion blasted inside the meteoroid and shattered it.

Chunks of iron and splashes of mercury were flung all around.

Ahriman managed to duck, and waited with his head flat against the sand.

He spotted the unthinkable — an upright, rectangular slab of ruby gemstone. It was about eight feet tall and covered with mercury, which poured slowly from the top, revealing a bas-relief of a lean, winged human figure. It appeared to be some kind of a warrior king, or maybe even a god of some sort. Ahriman slithered forward and raised his head slowly to get a better view and decipher it.

Upon closer inspection, he discovered that it was a depiction of a dagger-bearded man wearing an open bronze helmet and a long shawl, which extended to the ground. A strip of embroidery edged the shawl, running from the man's shoulders down to his feet. This indicated that he was a nobleman or a royal. His hands were open as though in a handshake, the fingers pressed tightly against each other. His elbows were bent, with his forearms pointing upward—either in military salute or cosmic greeting. Which of these, was unclear to Ahriman. The most significant and distinguishing part of the figure was the mysterious object that he carried on his helmet. The top of the helmet converged into a lyre-shaped vessel, composed of three sails. Each sail resembled a stretched triangle with a sphere above and below, a total of six empty spheres. "What do these spheres mean? Is it a code, or perhaps a riddle?"

Ahriman was puzzled. "More importantly," he asked himself, "Whose face is in the relief? Who *is* this man?"

Ahriman stared at the eerie object cautiously, anticipating that it would come to life and expecting another form of strike. He kept his distance but was distracted by the sound of the infant babbling. He looked at the crosses. The infant re-appeared and pointed at the statue. Ahriman heard a strange noise, and glancing back at the statue, he sensed a change. He slithered around the back of the slab and saw liquid gold flowing down the back. The back was flat, like a tablet. The cascading gold formed cuneiform script in the ruby, which gradually became legible. He read it as it appeared:

*"They are all living in slavery and ignorance.*

*They shall all live in liberty and enlightenment.*

*They are abandoned and divided.*

*They shall be united and empowered.*

*It will be the end of obscurity.*

*It will be the dawn of a golden sunrise.*

*It will be the dawn of the predominant inclination towards the principle of liberty.*

*It will be the dawn of the ultimate resolution to the bias of leadership.*

*It will be the end of credulity and the propensity for false faiths.*

It will be the end of bigotry and exploitation.

Three men. Three liberators. Three regulators will initiate the triangle of justice: investigation, revelation, implementation.

They will live in three different millennia. Three vessels consisting of six spheres: three births, three deaths.

All spheres will encapsulate the same soul: the Supreme Soul of the Solutionist. In each life, they will prevail in battle against the Lord of Darkness and Master of the Underworld, Ahriman.

In his first life, the Solutionist will be a virtuous king who unites, redeems, and rescues people from the four corners of the Earth. In his second life, he will be a rebel who will revolt against Ahriman's agents. He will be a revolutionary man who will teach the truth about us and expose Ahriman's lies.

In his third life, the Solutionist will be a combination of his two past lives: a rebel king.

Ahriman and his forces will be warned of their precarious, clandestine position on Earth, of their demonic influence, and their abuse of credulous mankind. Ahriman will receive two warnings in the Supreme Soul's first and second lives. Yet he will ignore them, and continue to occupy the planet, intoxicating mankind's mind and soul with his toxic elixir.

The mission of the Supreme Soul in his third life and last reincarnation shall not be limited to leading, regulating, and liberating. The Third Man will face a world infested with lies and corruption caused by Ahriman and his allies."

As Ahriman read, his eyes turned red with wrath.

*"The third man is the Solutionist. He will bring the day of retribution and frashokereti if Ahriman does not heed this warning and withdraw before his last reincarnation. Never again will Ahriman see the Earth and the Sun.*

*The best ammunition I have given to humans is their emotions. They are buried deep in their hearts, like magma in the earth.*

*The Solutionist will awaken a volcano that has slept for thousands of years, and he will direct the lava.*

*The Solutionist knows how to turn an abused woman into a ferocious and merciless warrior, and an orphan into a commander.*

*The Solutionist will summon an army of immortals, and in an act of justice, they will become Ahriman's punishers, breakers of his sword and annihilators of his elixir.*

*The Solutionist will raise the Temple of Fire and the Kingdom of Justice."*

The scripture ended and vanished. The frustrated Ahriman bared his fangs for the first time and emitted a deafening, diabolical hiss. The message vexed Ahriman gravely, to the point that his body violently reacted. On his head, small black wings began to flutter. Insect heads popped up all over his body. They were black locusts that progressively manifested themselves on the surface of his skin, flapping their wings. It almost seemed that his whole body was a composite of millions of black locusts. They had hideous faces and sharp, bloody teeth.

In a sibilant whisper, Ahriman said, "No mortal can punish Ahriman! I will utilize my elixir to punish the punishers!"

Ahriman's words were synchronized with the locusts: they all screamed in harmony, creating a single, thundering, echoing voice in the crater.

"We will hunt the hunters!"

He regained his composure, and the locusts receded. Ahriman undulated around the ruby to see if the relief had vanished, but it hadn't.

He noted again how the man's helmet converged into a lyre-shaped vessel composed of three sails, remembered the scripture's words, and compared it to the relief. *They will live in three different millennia. Three vessels, consisting of six spheres: three births, three deaths. All spheres will encapsulate the same soul.*

Ahriman reasoned that the image before him depicted the Solutionist. Each sail on his helmet represented a life or a millennium, and each empty sphere was a soul keeper. The more he thought about it, the more he grew to like the challenge that Ahuramazda had presented him with.

He had to think of a counter-attack. He knew that the message of Ahuramazda referred to his new elixir. He heard the baby again - crying this time. Ahriman reflexively looked up. The infant sat near the tomb door of the middle cross. Ahriman waited to see if he disappeared, but he didn't. The infant was there, sobbing relentlessly. He assumed the mother must have died during the delivery or the earthquake, or maybe she was in the tomb. Ahriman was troubled, thinking that perhaps this infant was the first man and keeper of the Supreme Soul. He decided to launch a preemptive strike. Despite the infant's apparent omnipresence, he thought, 'It shouldn't be *that* easy. It might be a trap.' There was only one way to solve the enigma.

Kill the infant!

Ahriman dashed out of the crater to ensnare the infant. He mounted the rocky cliff, assailed by a mixture of uncertainty and doubt about how tangible his prey was.

He ascended the cliff to the height of the tomb at the center cross and raised his head above the edge of the terrace.

His eyes turned green with awe.

Contrary to what he'd assumed from below, the baby wasn't an illusion.

He even had the remains of birth-blood on his body.

This was a real human infant who appeared to want to have his cord cut and be free, but could not do it himself, so he sat and wept.

The mother was nowhere to be seen or heard.

Ahriman knew the abilities of a human infant at birth. This particular infant could sit, which was extraordinary. He wanted to see his face. Ahriman changed his head color from black to exotic green and hissed, and the baby turned to gaze at him, seemingly amused to see a giant green python.

The infant became quiet and stared at him blankly, then turned around and giggled.

Ahriman was astounded and disappointed to see that the infant was not a boy. It was a lovely baby girl with big hazel eyes and light brown hair, covered with birth-blood and playing with her umbilical cord.

Ahriman glanced back cautiously.

A female infant could not be the Solutionist. Then who was she? She could be a trap. Was she a genuine human? He was reluctant to approach her. He slithered his head gently closer to her, but stayed at a discreet distance — anything might happen. The size of Ahriman's head compared to the baby's body was like an elephant compared to a kitten.

The laughing baby opened her arms toward Ahriman, and in her own gritty manner, showed a remarkable lack of fear as she crawled toward the python.

Ahriman marveled at her audacity but decided not to take any chances, and to terminate her. She was all alone after all.

He opened his mouth and moved slowly toward her.

When the infant saw his open mouth, staring protruding eyes, and two gigantic, sharp fangs, she stopped giggling, turned back, and began crawling toward the chamber.

Ahriman's teeth loomed over her whole body like two arches.

She was escaping, and there was not enough room on the ledge for him to slither around. He would have to take her from above while he could. He jumped up, lifting his head to ambush her vertically, like a goblet placed over an ant.

At the sight of his huge looming jaws, the petrified infant began screaming and crying hysterically.

It was too late; she was inside Ahriman's jaws.

He decided she was too small to bite, so he would swallow her whole.

The infant continued crying shrilly as Ahriman began to close his massive jaws on her.

Suddenly, a sharp wind struck her tear-bathed face.

Two wide, flapping wings loomed over Ahriman.

He did not want to let go of his prey to identify the predator.

He held the infant in the fork of his tongue.

As the baby shot a last desperate glance at the sky, two sharp talons reached into Ahriman's mouth and grabbed her. She was hauled out of his mouth and upward with such force that her umbilical cord was ripped from her belly, its blood splashing Ahriman's face. Looking up, Ahriman saw an oversized white gyrfalcon flying away beyond his reach, with the baby held safely in its claws.

Ahriman stared at the fast-disappearing figure in disbelief and despair.

One white feather lay on the ground. Gravely irritated, Ahriman sniffed it and then licked the umbilical blood off his face, tasting it. The feather belonged to a real bird, and the blood was true human blood. He supposed the falcon would have the infant for dinner. What baffled him was why Ahuramazda had allowed the falcon to eat her. What was her purpose?

Nothing was solved, and yet more questions were added. Only one aspect of the riddle had become clear: the baby wasn't the keeper of the Supreme Soul, as it was a girl. Ahriman was left with only one clue, the blood track of the mystery mother. He followed the blood trail left by the umbilical cord into the tomb chamber.

His enormous eye filled the entire entrance door as he peered inside, and to his astonishment, there was nothing within – not even a coffin. Just an empty chamber.

There was, however, one odd detail. Engraved in the front wall of the chamber was the number fifty-eight.

Ahriman did not know what to make of it. He looked away in aggravation. Defeated and dismayed, his body stiffened to the point that not even his rattle moved. His eyes were frozen on the sky.

Anger played across his face as he pondered the new puzzle. The Devil had been foiled by a female infant and a bird, and all he could think about was his ego that was wounded by such an insult. He decided to return to the crater and the celestial object.

On his way down, Ahriman had a new idea. He stopped and looked back at the cliff. He looked to the left and right of the central tomb chamber, to where the two other crosses and chambers stood. He could not leave the site without first inspecting them. Making his way back up to the tomb on the right, he looked inside. Again an empty chamber, again only a number, but this time it was thirteen. This now was a clue; if his guess was right, the third tomb would contain the number thirty-three.

Ahriman slithered excitedly across the cliff toward the third cross and looked inside the third tomb. Again there was an empty chamber, again a number on the same wall. He was right! One victory at last - it was *thirty-three*.

The new conundrum was the center cross, the one where the infant had been. What did fifty-eight mean? He looked back down at the crater. Maybe the statue had some encrypted inscription that could be deciphered?

Ahriman rushed back down to the crater and studied the figure of the winged man meticulously. After a long interval, he concluded that the wings of the falcon were a manifestation of the graven man's wings.

His thoughts turned to the Solutionist, whom he knew would come to unravel the snares of destruction that he, Ahriman, would set for mankind.

"But what kind of adversary would this Solutionist be?" he asked himself.

Surely, a reincarnated Supreme Soul concealed in a human body would hold the celestial statue of a demigod? And this demigod would have help from accomplices.

Maybe the infant and the falcon were part of the Solutionist's team? This thought excited him, and he began to rattle his tail. He pondered the problem until he matched the text with the figure and skeptically concluded, "A king, a rebel, and a rebel king. Three tombs, three numbers. So? I know the creator's codes of thirteen and thirty-three, but what is fifty-eight? Who is the infant, and why a female?"

Ahriman's irritation increased as he looked up to the center cross and mused about how close he had been to destroying the infant, ending the idea of the Solutionist altogether.

"Damn it! I'm not that invincible and smart after all."

This was the second worst day of his existence in over four million years, ever since Ahuramazda had decided to evolve *Ardipithecus ramidus* into Homo-sapiens and what was to become the human race.

He realized that this was neither the time nor the location to feel remorse about the past. His concern was the Solutionist and possibly three thousand years of war in the future.

"Maybe Winston could figure out the missing link between the statue, the bird, and the girl, he thought. But then I would have to explain my loss, which means revealing my failure."

Winston was the wise old leader of a company of Ahriman's underlings, whose opinion and experience he respected, but he was not prepared to expose any personal weaknesses to him. He heaved a deep sigh and decided on two countermeasures: first, he must take preemptive action by summoning the Demonic Council to consult his two top deputies, and second, he would reveal his master weapon that would last a thousand years - his infamous elixir.

———————————

Chapter **IV**

## THE **DEMONIC COUNCIL**

### The **Underworld**

---

**605 BC**

*A*fter his humiliating defeat by the gyrfalcon and the revelation of his worst nemesis yet, Ahriman evaluated the situation and considered it grave enough to summon the Demonic Council.

He slithered out of the crater, avoiding the cliff and the Citadel of the Immortals to be safe. After what had happened, he did not trust that area.

Deep in the desert, he stopped and stared at the sand beneath him.

His huge eyes bulged as he opened his enormous mouth and made a deafening hiss that blew the sands like a desert storm.

A drop of venom dripped from his fangs.

The venom fell to the ground and magically formed a hole that gradually widened into a circular depression in the shape of a pit.

As the pit continued to deepen, a shaft was produced, widening until it was as large as the mouth of a volcano.

Without hesitation, Ahriman flung himself into a wild dive, plummeting into the hole at a blistering speed.

Down he went, deeper and deeper.

As he fell, images started appearing around him. Stone statues of three-headed dogs and hundred-handed monsters covered the walls.

Ahriman's satanic aura brought the dead demons to life as he flashed past them. One by one, the dogs turned from stone to flesh and growled dreadfully.

The hundred-handed monsters also became undead, and they motioned to Ahriman like beggars.

As he fell further, he accelerated to near lightning speed.

The walls gradually changed from ochre to red.

He passed through the Earth's core, and the walls of the shaft were now covered with molten lava from which flames flickered and heat radiated. The hundred-handed monsters whimpered in torment and perpetual pain. Their burning arms struggled fruitlessly, reaching for Ahriman.

Through to the Earth's core, Ahriman began to decelerate as he approached the bottom of the shaft, which was the entrance to the Underworld, immediately opening into the Grand Hall Square.

It was a terrible place, deep and dank, full of creatures that crawled and crept and shirked. It was dark as the devil's soul itself.

As he advanced toward the Grand Hall, he could better hear the scrape of paws and the sound of screams coming closer and closer.

Then there it was, the Underworld. Ahriman's realm.

No gate, no gatekeeper.

The Grand Hall was a cathedral-like cave submerged in a dismal and murky atmosphere. It was somber, with a central dome made of salt crystal.

Hanging upside-down from the dome were countless human silhouettes with shredded skins, blue in color, with morose and remorseful facial expressions.

The dome looked like a massive plantation of upside-down, empty shells of corpses. A few had a peculiar element of metamorphosis about them. Some of the skins had started peeling away from their human shapes and had morphed into half-rat, half-human forms, whereas others had changed into what looked to be half-fox, half-human. Still others had turned into locusts. The peeling of flesh signified a rebirth inside the Underworld.

The Grand Hall was shaped like a colossal square cul-de-sac with a black cube-shaped temple at its end. Innumerable bizarre creatures crawled on the floor, either around or facing the temple, as if they were practicing a pilgrimage or a cult-like ceremony.

The windowless temple itself was a mystical monument. It was the height and depth of a tall palm tree. Its walls were fully draped in black fabric. It was built against the end of the cul-de-sac, with three façades that faced the Grand Hall Square.

At the center of the temple's front façade shone a silver-framed diamond eye. Inside the eye was a mysterious black oval stone, made of a lava-like material with an undulating surface. The black stone was the only opening into the temple. Underneath the diamond eye was a copper barrel on a small island surrounded by a ring of lava. It was filled with boiling blood.

The eye projected a diamond-shaped spotlight that sporadically lit the Grand Hall Square, illuminating a certain area and leaving the rest in darkness. The spotlight also revealed the identity of the creatures scurrying about in the semi-darkness. They were the

Ratollahs, the repulsive rats, the size of fat rabbits. They were predominantly brown, with banded individual hairs, giving them a multi-colored appearance. Some had black tails, but the majority had white tails. Their tails were unnaturally long, about four times the length of their bodies. They were all soaking wet in sweat.

The Ratollahs crushed and crawled over one another. Some of them fought while others, with blood dripping from their mouths and whiskers, cannibalized and scavenged the corpses of the dead ones. Their facial morphology was a fusion of caveman and rat.

Ahriman hissed loudly as he approached the Grand Hall. As one, the Ratollahs stopped and stared at him, frozen like deer caught in headlights. Unbidden and in unison, they moved aside to open a wave-shaped passageway and bowed. Then in an odd gesture, they coiled their tails on their heads like turbans.

Ahriman landed softly and slithered through the Ratollahs toward the temple. Abruptly he stopped, his eyes turning green. Slowly his head turned to the right and he stared at a dark, foggy tunnel, which entered the Grand Hall from that side. Dimly visible in the gloom, an army of faceless blue eyes approached.

They were well disciplined and sounded like four-legged creatures. Their paws marched at one hundred forty beats per minute, a product of their nature as highly mobile predators and skirmishers. The abundance of unidentified blue-eyed creatures was all that could be seen in the murky tunnel.

Ahriman slithered behind the temple.

The Ratollahs dispersed and ran very quickly to regroup and segregate themselves by tail color, around the temple in circular rows.

They all bowed down to the black stone and waited motionless, as if it were a ritual or a call to order.

All the while in the background was the sound of marching.

A moment passed. Black smoke came out of the black stone, shaping itself into Ahriman's head.

The salt crystal dome lit up suddenly and revealed the gathered demons.

There he was, the Lord of the Underworld, on his throne. He stared at his subjects.

The Ratollahs with white tails, being less important, positioned themselves on the right side of the temple out of Ahriman's direct line of sight, while the senior white-tailed Ratollahs sat in rows at the end of the hall.

The Ratollahs with black tails settled down in the straw in the front row facing the front façade of the temple, directly in front of Ahriman. After they had scurried about to position themselves, they once again coiled their tails ceremoniously into turban shapes on their heads.

The anonymous blue-eyed creatures still marched slowly toward the tunnel entrance to his left, finally coming into the light of the crystal dome. They were disclosed to be a skulk of white Foxploiters.

They were morphed, in a similar fashion to the Ratollahs, into half caveman and half-fox. They were four-legged Foxploiters – only their heads and necks had the mixed morphology of human and beast. Leading them was Winston, a stout Foxploiter the size of a grizzly bear. He had a triple chin that resembled a pelican's lower beak.

Winston was a cunning old Foxploiter who seldom spoke. When he did, it was to make a plan or draw up a resolution.

The Foxploiters perched themselves on Ahriman's left side, distancing themselves from the Ratollahs.

All the creatures bowed down to the black stone and sat on their hindquarters.

A long silence fell. All that could be heard was the boiling sound of the blood in the copper barrel.

Ahriman broke the silence in a low and calm voice. "Demons of the Underworld, I have called this extraordinary Demonic Council, as we have just received a threat. A grave phase of our existence is upon us—"

Ahriman was interrupted by a murmur of anxiety. He raised his voice. "We have received a notice to vacate Planet Earth from none other than Ahuramazda himself!"

A brasher mumbling began amongst both species.

"Silence!" Ahriman shouted in such a commanding voice that many hearts went cold. "There is nothing to fear."

He waited and then, gazing around calmly, said, "We are in danger! Or are we?"

He burst into mocking, thunderous laughter. His audience was preoccupied by the threat and fear clouded their eyes.

The Demonic Council was a force majeure assembly which occurred very rarely. The first and only other assembly had taken place four million years earlier, at the start of mankind's evolution, when *Ardipithecus ramidus* first began to walk upright in Africa.

Ahriman addressed his listeners in a resounding voice. "Ahuramazda laid the foundation for a new kind of soul, as solid as bedrock. It is my duty as Master of all Demons and Lord of the Underworld to pass on to you such wisdom and warning as I have acquired. From this council, we must gather our courage to find in ourselves the astuteness, willpower, and malevolence needed to implement a plan that I'd like to call the *final* solution to the human question."

The Ratollahs applauded, but the Foxploiters merely listened. Some of the white-tailed scavenger

Ratollahs who still had blood around their mouths and whiskers laughed and rubbed their fat bellies.

"We will undertake these seemingly insurmountable tasks. Not only will we *not* vacate the planet," he said, with increased vigor. "But we will become its sole masters."

He raised his voice enthusiastically. "Not only will we not let the Solutionist overcome human corruption and enlighten them, but we will enslave the humans completely."

The Foxploiters wondered who the Solutionist was and remained thoughtfully silent. The Ratollahs, who did not understand that part and only cared about human slavery, launched a second round of applause, screaming "Hear! Hear!", and even stamped their feet. The stamping was so powerful that it shook the surface of the boiling blood vessel, rippling the surface.

Ahriman narrowed his eyes and stuck out his tongue, dipping the forked tip into the reservoir and taking a good sip of blood.

Their excitement and jubilation made three old, large Ratollahs creep out of their holes. They were elderly black-tailed, senior Ratollahs.

Led by one called Momo, they sat in the front row on their hindquarters, listening.

Ahriman narrowed his eyes and glanced at them discreetly, waiting for the cheering to settle down. He then screamed in a booming voice, "Ahuramazda does not want us to derail or harm his newly-evolved creatures" his tone became heavy with contempt, "*the humans.*"

He chuckled mockingly. "Ahuramazda believes in them. He thinks of them as his masterpiece, that they could be intelligent, respectable, honorable, united, and independent... *I* am certain...." He paused and then cried in a high, thick voice emboldened by each word, "That they are credulous, gluttonous, corruptible, destructible, and stupid as *sheep*! Above all, easy to divide and rule over."

There were unanimous cries of "Hear! Hear!" and enthusiastic applause.

Ahriman waited for his audience to settle down before continuing. "The new soul will be their liberator, unifier, and regulator. He won't be a man, and he won't be a god. Ahuramazda called him the Supreme Soul, the Solutionist."

Attempting to transfer his energy to his disciples, he screamed with wrath, "My fellow demons, if we do not take his threat seriously, and if we do not take the lead in this battle—if we continue to allow men to occupy the surface of the planet—then this infested cave..." he looked around the Grand Hall before continuing with more venom and fury, "this sordid coffin, this lugubrious grave, this hot and rotten

Underworld, will become our *only* world. Our damnation will become our naked frailty, and our naked frailty will become our last identity."

The audience became morose, rumbled and growled.

Ahriman said rhythmically, articulating his words, "WE – DO – NOT – WANT – THAT!"

Everyone on the floor shook their heads simultaneously in support, and all their voices echoed, "NO, NO, NO!"

He glared penetratingly right into their eyes, and with words intended to pierce their minds, continued slowly, "The humans' best ammunition for war is their emotion. Supposedly it is hidden in their hearts like lava in a volcano's hearth. These are the words of Ahuramazda. The worst part of it is, the Solutionist summoned the abused women—" He paused, changed mood abruptly, and raised his voice, "Those whores will turn into furious warriors and overcome our army. The Solutionist will become our punisher, with an army of *immortals!* The question is: who can cause a sleeping volcano to erupt and turn female slaves into an army of immortals? Who?"

A general gasp of bewilderment and horror went up, followed by a deathly silence. The word "punisher" had alarmed everyone. Some Ratollahs visibly swallowed and fear shone in their eyes.

Ahriman shouted in high wrath, "Ahuramazda's tablet was an insult to me when it said: 'It will be the dawn of the predominant inclination towards the principle of liberty.' He looked at the Foxploiters 'It will be the dawn of the ultimate resolution to the bias of leadership." He looked at the Momo, 'It will be the end of credulity and propensity toward false faiths. It will be the end of bigotry and exploitation.' This is what we are all about. This means the end of us!" He paused and added with more vigor, "I will implement with my new elixir credulity through Momo, and exploitation through Winston – *indefinitely*! This is how we will own the planet, and this is why you Ratollahs and Foxploiters were summoned."

He sipped blood from the barrel. "Ahuramazda in his tablet threatens that 'three men, three liberators, three regulators will initiate the triangle of revelation, implementation and justice.'" a silence of fear reigned over the Grand Hall.

"What is to be implemented, Master?" asked Momo.

"Punishment, Momo! Punishment." Ahriman started shaking his rattle. The audience focused on him, as this was a sign of an important declaration. He stopped the rattle and shouted, "I, Ahriman, the Master of the Underworld, the Great Satan, and the Lord of all Evils, vow in this sacred temple of ours that we *will* find those three men in their own millennia and not only will we *kill* them, but we will either distort their legacy or erase it."

He stopped and stared at his puzzled audience. Contrary to what he expected, he did not receive an ovation, as they had absolutely no idea who those three men were. Ahriman continued, "What is to be investigated and revealed?" The Ratollahs universally shrugged. The Foxploiters were perplexed.

"His men will investigate us and reveal us to the humans, as we are rubbish. His implementation will be justice, and his justice is our punishment."

Ahriman added calmly to his terrorized audience, "I'd like to call our adversary the Demigod. Be assured that his supremacy is limited. The Demigod can travel through time using the same soul, but in three different bodies, only for a restricted period of three thousand human years. In his third incarnation, if we still exist physically on Earth..." Ahriman punched his words chillingly. "He shall *annihilate* us!"

All eyes protruded, and all hearts were gripped by a common fear.

Ahriman smirked, but his followers were stricken. The Ratollahs responded with a long, general, thundering sigh. The Foxploiters manifested their worry through their eyes.

"The Demigod knows everything that he has lived through in his previous two lives. His return won't be a normal reincarnation—"

Winston interrupted Ahriman. "What is a normal reincarnation, Master? Was ours normal?"

"Yes, your reincarnation was normal, Winston. The ultimate question that mankind must ask themselves is, 'What is our quest in life?' The answer to that question is found in their past lives, not the present. The mind of a human thinks and wants to live in the present. Out of this comes depression, greed, envy, and disappointment, depending on their failures or achievements. But the heart and reason want to follow the patterns of the past life, as only these two know the truth. All of you are here in the Underworld because this is where you belong. You all used to be human once, and I will…" Ahriman paused teasingly and did a 180-degree scan of his captivated audience before adding more energetically, "And I *will* make you human again!"

They hailed and greeted the idea deliriously with an outburst of thunderous applause.

Ahriman looked at them with pity, and thought to himself, 'Once a human, always a human. A healthy human can only appreciate his health when he is sick. He only appreciates his liberty when he is locked up, and he only appreciates being a human once he has turned into a demon in the Underworld.' He did not, however, share that thought with them.

"Quiet! Quiet!" he ordered.

Silence fell in the Grand Hall, and Ahriman went on, "The most important privilege of any human is to be a living being. Life is precious, and there is much to be done by each human. Those who wasted their lives didn't do what they should have done and didn't achieve what they should have achieved...they are the ultimate losers!

"You are not losers, because you are here in my kingdom. You will become human again. However, you will be demons in human skin. This is my supremacy over Ahuramazda and his frivolous rules. I am more forgiving than he is. His rules of reincarnation are distorted and unfair. My rules are fair.

"Now, to answer the fundamental question that has been tickling your brains forever: Where is Heaven, and who is included? Ahuramazda allows human souls to return and live a new life—a reincarnation based on their previous life's deeds. Those humans who respected his three rules in their past life will be granted a perfect world and a happy life afterward. What does this mean? They will live in Heaven, and Heaven is—" He stopped and observed their facial reactions. Their eyes grew bigger and their ears lifted.

"Heaven happens to be nowhere else, but Earth itself!"

A loud gasp of shock and puzzlement went up.

"Those who live in Heaven do not know it! Why not?"

Eyebrows rose.

He chuckled. "They will be fortunate and blessed from birth to death, and everything they touch will turn to gold. Happiness and love will always be around the corner, and life will smile on them day in and day out. They will often say, 'I'm living in a dream.' Or, 'I love my job.' Or, 'I have a great marriage.' Sometimes they complain, 'I'm bored, life is not challenging. I can obtain things that others dream of. Everything is easily accessible.' This is living in Heaven because *Heaven is a boring place.*

"Ahuramazda grants three purposes to a human's life, and those who have achieved at least two out of the three are in Heaven. The first is professional success. This means to have an occupation that they are not only passionate about, but are also excellent at. The second purpose is the toughest one, finding a compatible spouse that makes them happy and *complete.* A relationship that lasts until both die and even beyond, because those humans who truly find a perfect love, even after their second half dies, still live on with the memory of love. But, as I have said, love is the most difficult purpose to achieve."

Ahriman paused, then added, "The third purpose is that their children grow up to become respectful, loyal, and successful. Humans who achieve these three purposes live in Heaven's heartland. Two out of three puts them in Heaven's hallway.

"Question! Why do some humans get to have all that? Only because they had respected Ahuramazda's three rules in their past life. This is why I call him unjust. Now, let's talk about *you*."

Some of the Ratollahs started to rub their forepaws excitedly, as at last after his long explanation about the people in Heaven, it was their turn to learn why they were in the Underworld in the first place.

Ahriman continued, "The second group is you, my people." He paused pensively. "Actually, you are the third group. The first group is the Heaven people. The second is the probation people, and the third is you in the Underworld." He stuck his tongue into the blood barrel.

"The second group consists of those who violated the three rules in their first life. They will be reincarnated and live a very hard second life of a *suspended sentence*. The worst part is, they will have no clue about the misdeeds of their past life. Some do not even believe in reincarnation. They complain that their life is hard and that they are unlucky, doomed, and miserable. In their work, no matter how talented they are, or how deep they invest themselves in it, results will be inconclusive, and there will be no compensation! A masturbatory, pathetic, and fruitless professional and personal life. They wish for it to come to an end, but suicide is not an option. They fantasize about being put to sleep for years, just so they can get a break from their miserable lives, but they can't! Consequently, they project negativity and pessimism and can't even find a friend. They have a very poor sex life and are often single. Everything that they touch turns to shit, and they are often depressed and unhappy — all without knowing why.

"Ahuramazda is making them pay the price for the aggressions and crimes of their previous lives. Ironically, that misery is their last chance to accept being good and to respect Ahuramazda's three ridiculous rules: *good deeds, good words, good thoughts.* During that reincarnation, that second life is a period of probation. It can either be a bridge to Heaven or a diving cliff to here. Even though they are granted a second chance to respect Ahuramazda's principles, they must pay the price for the misdeeds of their first life, which makes their existence even harder. Cheating, lying, stealing and killing bring them here. Now here is their dilemma: they must learn to be good while having a bad life."

He grinned diabolically and affirmed, "By default, most fail."

Ahriman dipped his tongue into the blood reservoir and then added in a quiet, but firm voice, "Guess what?"

He paused, teasing his transfixed audience by taking his time to savor the boiling blood, and then finally added, "We can't blame them. They are going to have extremely difficult lives. Most doors will be constantly closed to them. They will go through relentless calamities that they play no part in. Misery will fall into their lives like a hair into soup. Where do all these hardships funnel them?"

Ahriman now faced a speechless, morose audience who knew the answer, but didn't want to accept it. He gazed at their ice-cold eyes and sullen faces, and he laughed a devilish laugh. "Here! To the Underworld. Unless they can swim inexhaustibly against the river flow. They will be lonely, miserable, rejected, and unhappy. They will live precariously and sickly, or they will bring sick children into the world, and they won't realize that it is Ahuramazda who *made their time on Earth a living hell*. His plan is to see whether or not they can thrive through tribulation, and remain honest and faithful in that tough environment without taking their own lives or engaging in new misdeeds. If they don't crack, and they follow his three rules, by about the age of fifty, the curses will be lifted and doors will be opened for them until they die.

"After they die, Ahuramazda will grant them an easy and fruitful life in their next reincarnation. However, if before they reach the age of fifty they break or fall for my temptation, violate his three rules, or commit suicide, directly or indirectly, then according to reincarnation cosmic codes, there is no mercy. *There will not be a third chance!*"

As Ahriman emphasized his last words, a female Foxploiter behind Winston shed a single tear. She had just realized what eternal damnation meant.

Ahriman didn't even look at her. Instead, he yelled, "Forty days after they die, their souls inhabit three-headed dogs, then hundred-handed monsters, and then gradually they make their way down to the Underworld where, as you can see…" He gestured his head toward the dome. The eyes of his audience followed and gazed up at the flayed skins.

Ahriman continued, "They are hung upside down in their own deflated and shredded skins until finally, in their senior stage, according to my rules, they are reborn as Ratollahs, Foxploiters, or locusts and belong to me for eternity. As you *all* do!"

A general mournful sigh went up, and their faces showed deep desolation.

A venomous grin cast itself across Ahriman's face. "It is rare that a demon-minded human turns virtuous. Some will try during their reincarnation, but as we all know, bad humans do three things subconsciously: the first is to do harm to others, the second is to become envious of the happiness and success of others, and the third is to enjoy watching others fail. This is a habit that you bring with you even here, when you cannibalize one another. Do you know why?" Ahriman answered his own question. "Because the pain and agony of others is your ecstasy and glory. It's what you crave. It's nourishing to make others miserable and to watch them suffer."

Ahriman and some of his audience, especially the cannibal Ratollahs with the bloody whiskers, burst into hysterical laughter. Some didn't laugh. For the first time, they grasped why they were in the Underworld and that they would stay there in perpetuity.

They even regretted not taking advantage of the probationary period and the second chance in their reincarnation to be good. They understood that they were now trapped for eternity and that Ahriman would never release them. In the best-case scenario, he would use them for his own benefit. They were sad and missed being human yet again. They understood that

Ahriman didn't care about them and became despondent at the realization.

Ahriman read their thoughts. "But here is the good news! In your second life, when you violate the good deed rules and come to me, that doesn't mean that I will keep you here forever. I do own your soul, which I put into the body of a rat, locust, or fox. However, I also have the power to reincarnate you. Only with me, you will be *evil.*"

He said the word "evil" with a fiendish grin on his face, and a spark flashed in his eyes. "You will be evil, but with a mission that I will give to you. Anyone who stands in your way must perish!"

He paused, and his voice became more forceful. "No exceptions! No mercy! If necessary, you will kill your own mother, innocent people, their children, and even domestic animals so that you can set an example. You shall be demons in human bodies. I will grant you the power of ruling and leading other humans to their own destruction and decay, into the abyss."

Injecting more vigor into his voice, he said, "They will follow you like sheep to the slaughter, and only then will you comprehend and appreciate that it is *good* to be evil!"

At that point, Ahriman received a tumultuous round of unanimous applause from the Ratollahs and

Foxploiters who cried, "Hear! Hear!" They all hoped that they could still be reincarnated and again become human, albeit under Ahriman's umbrella. They shrugged and thought, 'As long as we go back to life and become human again, we don't need to worry about Ahuramazda's rules.'

Ahriman was happy with their reaction. "This was the answer to Winston's question, and also what you have all been wondering about for the past four million years. Now you know. However..."

He took a fresh sip of blood. "This council was not assembled to examine and analyze the laws of reincarnation and its cosmic codes, but for the reincarnation of one specific soul, the Supreme Soul. Based on what I have learned from the tablet, the Demigod is an exceptional human—a wonder of Ahuramazda's creation. He knows exactly who he has been in his past lives. He uses all the knowledge, experience, and leadership skills earned throughout three millennia to get through to all people from all nations. He can communicate with both the dead and the living and reach out to everyone globally throughout time."

Here, no one even gasped, but thousands of Ratollahs' jaws dropped simultaneously.

Winston, however, whispered admiringly to himself, "Three thousand years of wisdom and connection is hard to top."

Ahriman swiftly turned his head to Winston and gave him a warning look. "The dead humans share information with him, and the living ones want him to lead them, despite the fact that he speaks a different language, that he is not one of them, and that he was born in a different country—a foreigner. Yet they feel that he was one of them in his past life, and that he has returned to finish his job. He seduces them with his magnetism and charisma. He galvanizes them to such a degree that they would follow him through fire. This is what worries me the most: his ability to communicate and influence.

An even bigger menace is his accomplices."

Ahriman paused to think before reluctantly adding, "I have no idea who they are, how much power they have, or where they are. They could be anything. A human, an animal, a country, energy, nature, destiny, a bird—"

"A bird?" Winston interrupted him.

Ahriman paused and the image of the gyrfalcon flashed before his eyes. He refocused, but it was too late. Winston had already detected the lie in Ahriman's face. He suspected that information had been censored.

"Yes, a bird or…or Ahuramazda himself," Ahriman replied. "Or even a dream—I have no way of knowing—"

"You have no way of knowing? You, the Great Satan and the Lord of all Evils, have no way of knowing? This is truly alarming, Master."

Ahriman either wasn't upset or managed to contain his anger, as the locusts on his body did not flap their wings. After a long pensive pause, Ahriman, still keeping his head inside the black stone throne, said calmly, "I have no way of knowing who we are up against exactly, because he has not even been born yet. This is why we are having this Demonic Council, to *prevent* his birth."

"What *do* you know Master?" insisted Winston.

Ahriman, for the first time, heaved a deep sigh that panicked the entire floor. "I know we are up against a being that comes from the uncharted, utmost realms. Someone who is exceptional and surreal. The Demigod must be a complex creature made of man, animal, and nature, imbued with a Supreme Soul and commissioned by Ahuramazda to be the Solutionist. Our punisher."

Ahriman examined their facial expressions from his lofty position with its panoramic view of his Grand Hall. To his right was the semi-circle of Ratollahs, and to his left was the other semi-circle of

Foxploiters. Not a single eye blinked. Ahriman faced a petrified audience that had literally stopped breathing. All eyes were fixed on him. With a head gesture, motioning to the left and then to the right, he emphasized the enormity of the adversary.

"He will fuse all human minds into one idealistic network against us. He will try to educate, enlighten, and motivate them. We, however, shall keep them divided, insecure, morose, and oblivious—at all times."

His audience, particularly the Ratollahs, became firmly convinced that the Solutionist was a robust nemesis, and that they might never get out of the Underworld. They wondered if Ahriman had been lying to them all along. Fear crept over their bodies, starting from the legs. The energetic stamping feet weakened, and some clutched their stomachs.

A mood of dismay wafted across the assembly.

Ahriman took his eyes off the Foxploiters and addressed the Ratollahs directly this time.

"I will give you a weapon that loads itself perpetually with toxic ammunition, which will cripple a human's mind. In addition, it will have no antidote. Nobody will ever outgun you, not even the Demigod. My dear demons, I've named it…."

Ahriman stopped for another teasing pause.

They waited. Silence fell.

He enjoyed extending the anticipation. All eyes were focused on his sealed mouth as they wondered what he was waiting for.

Winston knew this trick. Ahriman was preparing his audience for his magic weapon - building up the expectation and excitement. Winston was preoccupied with the Demigod and not particularly enthusiastic about the new weapon. He was disturbed by the fact that Ahriman, so far, had not given them any information about how, why, and where he had gotten Ahuramazda's tablet.

So he decided to be the audacious one and break the silence. "What is the name of your weapon, Master?"

"At last, one smart question, Winston," replied Ahriman with a satisfied smile. Then he added proudly, again addressing only the Ratollahs, "I call it the Elixir of Ignorance. It will direct a human's mind. They will follow you blindly and respect you unconditionally. It will help you harness the power of humans' thoughts and paralyze their faculty of understanding and ability to reason."

The Ratollahs glanced at each other absolutely perplexed, and wondered how humans would ever respect them, let alone follow them blindly.

Ahriman continued, "I know you think it sounds unlikely and you're wondering how you could possibly control a human's mind, but we've done this before. Momo here, was reincarnated by me 1200 years ago."

Ahriman turned to Momo. "Remember Momo?" Momo nodded proudly with a big smile on his face.

Winston was annoyed by the whole subject and wondered where Ahriman was taking this, and why he had avoided the subject of the Solutionist.

Ahriman went on even more vigorously, "When Momo was in power, he did all the killing that needed to be done in order to implement my elixir. After slaughtering all the men, he sent Phineas to kill all the *women and children* of the Midianites, the very tribe who adopted him as a refugee. They gave him a wife and a new life safe from the law, since Momo was on the run after killing an Egyptian officer. Remember, Momo?"

"Yes, Master. I killed him good, didn't I?" said Momo.

"You killed everyone very well, Momo. I'm proud of you, which is why I have a much bigger plan for you in your next reincarnation and there will be much more killing this time. Which brings us to my new weapon, and the second reason of this Demonic Council. But first, let us diagnose what went wrong with my last elixir, to avoid making the same mistakes twice. I invented three characters: Lilith, Adam, and Eve. Lilith was the antagonist, since she was an independent woman who believed in equal rights between *man* and *woman*." All the Ratollahs suddenly burst into hysterical laughter. Ahriman grinned.

"I needed to lay the foundation of separation between humans in their very core. I created a sex war, and fragmented their liaison, as long as humans used my elixir. I staged the concept of Adam as the role model of all men, and two villains, which were his wives, both with diabolical thoughts, acts, and ideas. Adam was developed as a dominant man who needed a submissive wife, so he complained to the fake god, and he sent Adam a new wife, whose name was Eve. She was, as he wanted a woman to be, subdued and docile. We implemented the culture of *obedient* women through Lilith's punishment, and introduced Eve as the mother of all humans. We told them that Lilith was turned into wind, because of her insubordination to her man. However, we couldn't let Eve off the hook and make her look perfect, so we branded her as a wicked woman who fell for the forbidden fruit.

"Naturally, we didn't tell them the truth; how Ahuramazda had given them the faculty of physical and intellectual evolution. We wanted them to remain stupid so they would follow us. The truth about what happened four million years ago, when *Ardipithecus ramidus* first walked upright and became the real human ancestor, is absurd. Obviously, man cannot relate to an ape, but he can relate to a dominant Adam, who suffered because his first wife was rebellious, and his second wife's greed became the cause of their expulsion from Heaven. Not only did we teach them a lie, but we also banned the truth. But then women started asking questions about why Lilith was punished, when all she asked was that man and woman be equal. Why did Eve take the blame, when Adam could have said 'no' to the apple?"

Ahriman sipped some blood and added, "My biggest problem with humans is women."

He emphasized in a hoarse voice, "I don't *like* them. They are analytical, responsible, and inquisitive. Men are easier to manipulate. They have ego, and ego is good for us. Ego is what we need to cloud their minds and cause wars. Using their ego, we sold them the idea of Adam and his supremacy. We gave him the right to have two wives. We built the culture of patriarchy."

Although the Ratollahs didn't know what patriarchy meant, they liked the sound of it and simply nodded. Ahriman continued, "If Adam was better than Eve, then men in general are better than women." The Ratollahs applauded unanimously, the Foxploiters didn't.

"Momo *formalized* this doctrine by implementing and enforcing the idea and concept of Lilith and Eve as the villains. Momo did a brilliant job of introducing our elixir and imposing *it* with the power of the sword."

Ahriman sighed sullenly and added, "The problem arose after they killed my Momo – his *disgraceful* own people! Momo was killing too many, and at one point they said, 'To hell with him, let's just kill the son of a bitch, and get rid of him.'

"Remember, Momo?" he asked in a sympathetic tone, and looked at Momo, whose facial expression shifted from a proud winner to a sad victim. He nodded with pouted lips.

Ahriman maintained eye contact with Momo and continued, "You were standing by the hill, and the next thing you knew, they were stabbing you in the back and slaughtering you! But that's fine, Momo, don't you worry, Momo. I will send you back, and you will take revenge on the people of your first life. A war of elixirs."

Ahriman stopped his one-on-one and looked back at the whole hall, "The problem was that Momo's people, those so-called devotees, changed our methodology. Instead of imposing the elixir as Momo did by force, they decided to transfer it by a mother bloodline, which limited the number of our followers and shriveled away my area of influence to the extent that it became useless. This new—"

"Regardless, Master," interrupted Winston. "Momo's people from his past life are filthy, selfish, and cheap, to the point that they are hated by everyone, everywhere, throughout time. What use do we have for more of them representing us?" The Foxploiters confirmed their support of their leader with cries of "Hear! Hear!"

"Quiet in the hall!" ordered Ahriman, then looked at Winston. "We are not in the business of *likability*, Winston. We are in the business of use and abuse and *destruction*. For your information, Momo's people of his next life will be much worse and even more hated than his first-life people. This new elixir that I am formulating will be administered neither by blood, nor by choice or campaign, but by *mandate*. You'll *make* them drink my elixir or you'll cut their throats, with a double pointed sword - *just like my tongue*!" He burst into a psychotic laugh, with the Ratollahs joining in.

"There is no use for a human who does not convert to my new elixir. Unless they are on the Foxploiters' side, in which case they won't be converted, but will help to administer it."

A general gasp went up from the Foxploiters and from the Ratollahs in the front rows, which were filled with black-tailed Ratollahs.

"I will reincarnate Momo. I will turn him into a holy leader, and you, my beloved Ratollahs, are all going back as well."

The white-tailed Ratollahs in the back rows started to applaud and cheer. Ahriman whirled his head to face the Foxploiters. "Winston, you and all your Foxploiters must learn to love the Ratollahs and cooperate with them. I don't like this conflict between Foxploiters and Ratollahs. You are all scavengers here, nobody is better than anybody else. There is no good or bad amongst us, we are all evil. With Momo's guidance and leadership, armed with my new elixir and with Winston's wise and the Foxploiters' art of exploitation, we *will* dominate planet Earth *unconditionally*."

"This time, like before, your identity will remain unknown to the humans. Maybe only the Demigod will be able to detect your demonic soul. And if he attempts to reveal your secret, your followers will prosecute him for blasphemy and heresy for comparing you to rats."

The Ratollahs wondered what kind of sorcery Ahriman was up to. How could the Demigod be punished for calling a rat a rat? Ahriman gave his habitual devilish grin, flicked his tongue in and out in a serpentine manner, and then dipped it into the blood reservoir. He added in a hollow voice, "Be patient, my little demons. I will give you the alchemy of the *poisoning* elixir, and a new identity with it."

He then whirled his head to his left and gazed at the Foxploiters.

"Our mission statement: global demonic domination!"

The Foxploiters cried out euphorically, "Hear! Hear!" Paw-tapping began amongst them.

Winston did not react. He listened serenely to Ahriman.

"You cannot content yourselves with the Underworld to fighting among yourselves and cannibalizing each other. You must take over the Earth and dwell upon it, not as Ratollahs or Foxploiters, but humans. Not humans who will obey Ahuramazda's three useless rules, but as humans who will obey *me*. Once you become human again, hand-in-hand, you Foxploiters and you Ratollahs will encircle the planet and expand my serpentine power until it stretches itself around the Earth. It must envelop the world and plunge it into the chaos of doomsday: corruption, starvation, exploitation, injustice, mendacity, lies, slaughtering of the innocents, subjugation of women, and even the destruction of the planet as a whole. With my elixir, and under your influence and authority, your followers will bring doomsday to themselves, and only then our campaign of total annihilation of mankind will have begun!"

"Hear! Hear!" cried the Foxploiters.

The morale of the Ratollahs rose as Ahriman burst into a loud laugh, which was drowned out by a spirited round of applause mixed with Foxploiters' and Ratollahs' laughter and cheers.

"After we terminate the humans, we will aim at Ahuramazda himself—" He paused. A hellish fire burned in his eyes, and he sucked as much hot air as he could into his chest before he shouted enthusiastically, "If we can take over the Earth, we can surely also take over the Overworld."

There was a tremendous uproar of applause and paw stamping. Their excitement and jubilation brought a smug smile of glory to Ahriman's face. Momo was applauding, but Winston was not. Ahriman waited for the applause and cheering to die down.

Then he said, "Only at that time will I own the universe. The globalization of my authority will be run by you, my demons!"

The whole floor was jubilant and in a state of wild ecstasy, nearly out of control in their elation and enchantment.

Momo and Winston were the only ones not cheering.

Winston observed in silence and waited for the uproar to calm down.

Order returned at last. The Foxploiter leader attempted to speak, but a white-tailed Ratollah cut him short.

"Does that mean, Master, that we will all become human again?"

Ahriman ignored the question since it came from a common Ratollah, unworthy of a reply. In general, he only spoke to the group leaders, especially in the Demonic Council, which was a highly formal assembly.

Ahriman's tongue flicked out. The Ratollah that had asked the question panicked and stepped back, terrified, but the other Ratollahs held him. They expected Ahriman to feed him to his locusts as punishment for speaking directly to the Great Satan. It was a brief, tense moment, but Ahriman merely put his tongue into the reservoir and took another sip of boiling blood.

Winston waited before inquiring in a resonant voice, "When will he manifest himself, Master? The Solutionist?"

Ahriman left the subject of the Solutionist behind, preferring to equivocate and talk now about the elixir and his plans for universal dominance. He replied reluctantly under his breath and in a rasping voice, "We don't know. But I will know when it happens."

He glanced back at the Ratollahs and raised his voice more enthusiastically. "Now, let's talk about my elixir and its implementation by you, my dear Ratollahs."

Winston wasn't content and persisted, "What other indication has Ahuramazda given you, Master? You mentioned a tablet. Where was it or where did it come from? How did you discover it?"

Winston irritated Ahriman with his curiosity. He heaved an exasperated sigh to show his annoyance.

Ahriman had no desire to explain his humiliating defeat by the gyrfalcon. Nonetheless, one of the purposes of the Demonic Council was to consult his top deputies, Winston and Momo. Indeed, he often considered Winston to be the second brightest mind in the Underworld after himself. He was analytical and enquiring, and maybe he could answer all of the questions that were left unanswered from the Citadel of the Immortals. After losing his prey, how could he truthfully brief them without damaging his credibility? But if he withheld the truth, then how could they help him solve the conundrum?

Dilemma. Dilemma. Dilemma.

Ahriman thought, 'I am the lord of lies. I should be able to brief my subjects on the truth, marinated with just a touch of falsehood. However, Winston is an old Foxploiter and I cannot fool him.'

While Ahriman pondered, Winston, with an impatient expression, started to scratch the back of his ear with his forepaw. His intense interest had been transmitted across the whole floor, and as one, the Ratollahs and Foxploiters pondered the origin of the tablet. Ahriman saw this in their eyes, and considered.

Winston stepped forward and asked more disturbing questions, "I also wondered why, amongst all creatures, our great Master singled out *a bird*? Does the tablet involve a bird? Does the bird have to do with the Tower of Silence? In that case, it means you found the tablet in the Aryan kingdom and—"

Ahriman interrupted him angrily, "Alright! Enough with the cross-examination! How dare you – you old fat fox, question me? I shall reprimand you for your insolence!"

Ahriman narrowed his eyes and stared furiously at Winston. The Foxploiters were proud that their chief had listened and connected the dots. The Ratollahs expected the wings of wrath to begin to flap from Ahriman at any moment and that the resulting swarm of locusts would eat Winston to the bone. As for Winston, he knew Ahriman spoke with a forked tongue, deliberately saying one thing and doing another.

He waited stoically for his answer. All eyes were waiting for Ahriman's reaction.

———————

To be continued…

Please visit KayvanD.com and enter your email address in the author's guestbook to receive information about his' forthcoming books.

www.ingramcontent.com/pod-product-compliance
Lightning Source LLC
Chambersburg PA
CBHW020412150626
46554CB00013B/834